ZOO CREW

Tiger Twins

Written by Brenda Scott Royce

Illustrated by Joseph Wilkins

JOLLY
FiSH
PRESS
Mendota Heights, Minnesota

Book design by Sarah Taplin
Illustrations by Joseph Wilkins (Beehive Illustration)

Published in the United States by Jolly Fish Press, an imprint of North Star Editions, Inc.

First Edition
First Printing, 2022

This is a work of fiction. Names, characters, places, and incidents are either the product of the author's imagination or are used fictitiously, and any resemblance to actual persons living or dead, business establishments, events, or locales is entirely coincidental.

Library of Congress Cataloging-in-Publication Data (pending)
978-1-63163-624-0 (paperback)
978-1-63163-623-3 (hardcover)

Jolly Fish Press
North Star Editions, Inc.
2297 Waters Drive
Mendota Heights, MN 55120
www.jollyfishpress.com

Printed in the United States of America

TABLE OF CONTENTS

CHAPTER 1

Nursery Days

"Good morning, Junior Volunteers!" Luis said. He was the volunteer coordinator at Mountain Bluff Zoo. Luis was waiting near the entrance when Micah Draper and Katy Nichols arrived.

The two friends were wearing their matching safari vests. The vests had "VOLUNTEER" printed on the back. Micah and Katy waved to Luis.

"Today, you'll be helping out in the nursery," Luis told them.

"That's where they take care of animal babies," Katy told Micah. Her mother was a zookeeper. So, Katy spent a lot of time at the zoo.

"Awesome," Micah said. "Baby animals are so cute and cuddly."

Luis walked Micah and Katy to the nursery. He introduced them to Javier, the keeper on duty. Javier's big eyes and bushy brows reminded Katy of an owl. "Nice to meet you!" he said,

bringing the kids inside. Luis waved goodbye and returned to his office.

"How can we help?" Micah asked. Then he looked around the nursery. His smile faded. "Where are the babies?"

"There aren't any," Javier said. "Isn't it great?"

Katy looked around the large, cheery space. There were several incubators and cages. But they were all empty. "I'm confused. Why aren't there any baby animals here?" She put both

hands on her hips. "And why are you so happy about it?"

"All of the zoo's babies are with their mothers," Javier said. "That's why I'm happy. We only get babies that are sick. Or babies whose mothers can't properly care for them. So, we have to be ready. The nursery must always be clean and well-stocked. That's where you two come in."

"We're going to help clean?" Micah said. "But I wanted to take care of baby animals."

Javier patted him on the back. "Not today. Who knows what tomorrow will bring?"

CHAPTER 2

Cleaning's No Fun

When their volunteer shift ended, Micah's father drove them home. He peppered Micah and Katy with questions along the way.

"It was pretty boring," Katy said. "We scrubbed and cleaned all day."

"I didn't even get to take any animal pictures." Micah tapped the camera in his vest pocket.

"And I didn't have time to draw,"

Katy said. "When we finished cleaning, we did something called inventory. That's where we just counted all the supplies."

"Sounds kind of like my job," Mr. Draper said.

"But you fight fires," Micah protested.

"Not every day," his father said. "Sometimes there are no fires to put out. Then we take care of the trucks and the station. That way, we're always ready." He pulled to the curb in front of Katy's house. "Inventory may be boring, but it's important."

"I guess so." Katy reached for the door handle. "Thanks for the ride."

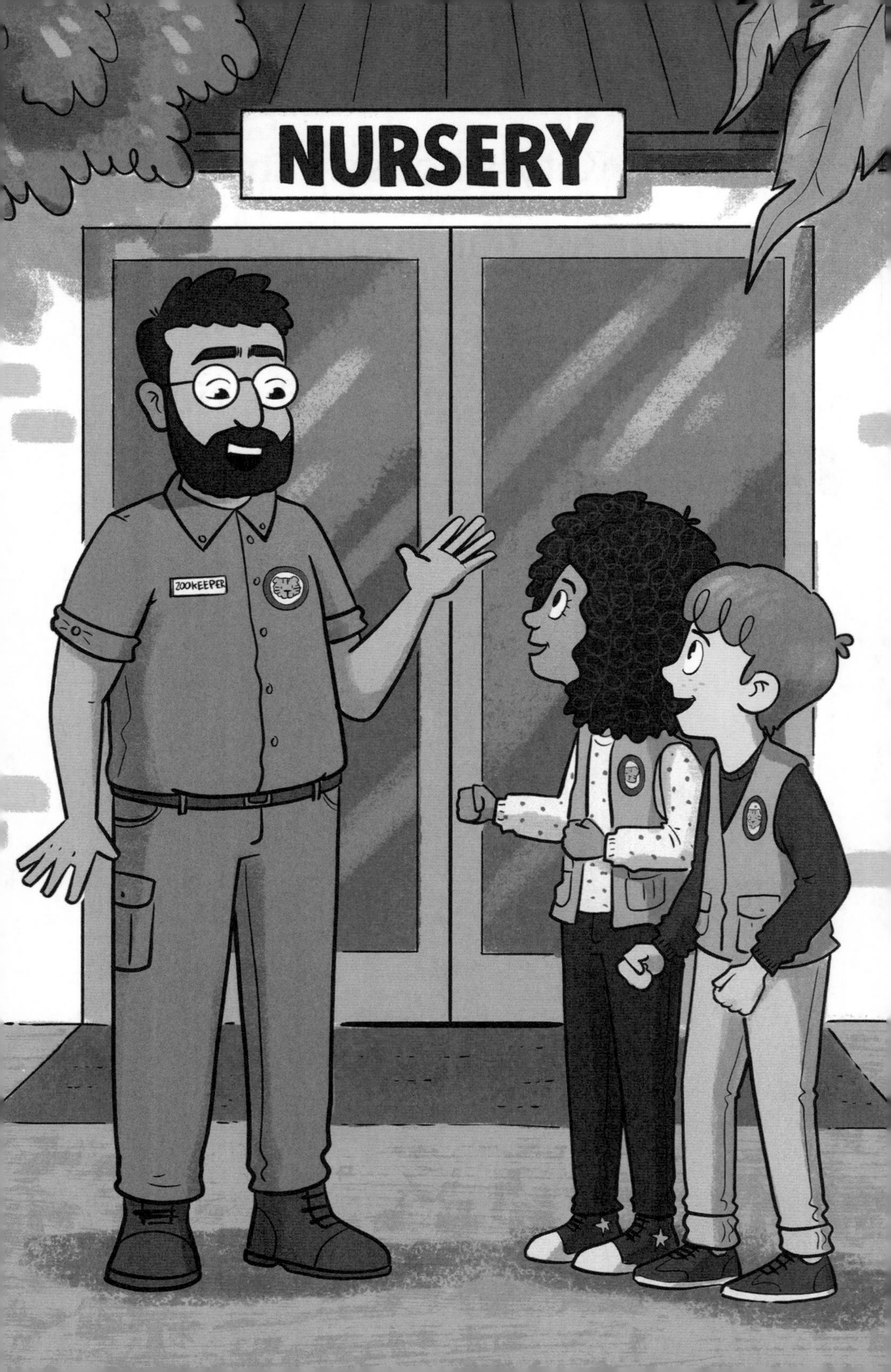
NURSERY
ZOOKEEPER

CHAPTER 3

Feeling Torn

Javier met the kids at the nursery the next morning. He had big news. "Lulu the tiger will give birth any day now."

Micah pumped his fist in the air. "Awesome!"

"Will the cubs come to the nursery?" Katy asked.

"Not if Lulu is able to care for them. She's never had cubs before. So, the keepers and veterinarians will be watching closely." Javier pointed to a computer on the counter. "Why don't you two research tiger cubs? The more you learn, the better prepared you'll be. Just in case we have to help out."

Micah hurried to the computer. He began typing in keywords. "Tigers usually have two or three cubs at a time," he read aloud.

"Wow," Katy said, writing in her notebook. "So, Lulu might have twins?"

"Or triplets!"

Katy continued her research at home that night. She read everything she could find online about tiger cubs. She took notes in the notebook she always brought to the zoo. Even after she crawled into bed, she was still reading about tigers.

Katy's mother appeared in her doorway. "Lights out, sweetie. Tomorrow's a school day."

Katy closed her notebook. "I hope Lulu doesn't go into labor during the week. I want to be there when it happens." She crossed the fingers of both hands. "And I super-duper hope that she can't take care of her cubs! That way, they'll go to the nursery."

Katy's mother frowned. "I'm glad you're excited to help, but . . ." She trailed off.

"What's wrong, Mom? You look sad."

"I was remembering the day you were born. It was the best day of my life." She leaned down and kissed Katy's forehead. "But that's partly because I was able to take care of you. If I wasn't, I would have been very sad. I hope Lulu can take care of her cubs. All mothers deserve that chance."

Now it was Katy's turn to frown. She wasn't sure what to wish for.

CHAPTER 4

Tiger Cubs

The next Saturday, Javier was grinning outside the nursery. He waved as Micah and Katy approached.

"You look happy," Micah said. Then he frowned. "That must mean the nursery is still empty."

The keeper chuckled. "Actually, we do have one little fellow. He will be staying with us for a few days."

Katy gasped. "Is it a tiger cub?"

"No. Lulu hasn't had her babies yet."

Micah hurried inside. He peered into the only occupied cage. "It's a . . . prickly thing!"

"A porcupine," Katy said. "It's so tiny."

Javier nodded. "He's one of three porcupines that were born last week. The keeper noticed he wasn't gaining weight like his siblings. So, we need to keep an eye on him. We need to make sure he eats."

He opened a cabinet where baby bottles of various sizes were lined up neatly. "Good thing you two helped us stock up on our supplies."

He picked a small bottle and filled it with formula. Then he handed it to Micah.

Micah held the bottle up to the

porcupine's mouth. But the baby didn't respond.

"Give the bottle a little squeeze," Javier said. Micah did. They heard soft sucking noises as the baby began to drink.

Then Katy took a turn with the bottle. "He's hungry," she said, smiling.

When the baby stopped drinking, Javier held the bottle up to the light. "Almost empty. Great!" He made a note in the animal's chart.

The phone rang, and Javier answered it. "It's time," he told the kids when he hung up the phone. "Lulu's in labor!"

Javier, Micah, and Katy arrived at the tiger building and went around to the back. Javier opened a door marked "STAFF ONLY."

"Lulu's night quarters are just ahead," he said. "We can watch through the window. Keep your voices down. We don't want to disturb her."

They reached a large room. It had a thick glass divider. On the other side,

they could see the tigers. Lulu was lying on her side, breathing heavily. Nestled next to her was a tiny cub. The cub's eyes were still closed.

The veterinarian, Dr. Chu, crouched down next to the window. "Come on, Lulu," she said.

Jennie, the tiger keeper, was pacing back and forth. She told them the first cub appeared healthy. Now they were waiting on the second to be born.

"Shouldn't you be in there with her?" Micah asked the vet.

Dr. Chu shook her head. "Only if something goes wrong. Mama tigers give birth in the wild without our help. They do it in zoos too."

"It's not safe to go in with her," Jennie added. "A mother tiger will attack anyone she thinks is a danger to her cubs."

Minutes later, the second cub made its way into the world. There were smiles all around. Lulu groomed both cubs, licking them from head to toe.

"I read that the licking motion is important," Katy said. "It stimulates the cubs' lungs. It helps them start breathing on their own."

"That's right, Katy," Dr. Chu said. "And it looks like Lulu knows just what to do."

"I read that tiger cubs are born blind," Micah added. "Their eyes won't open for a week or two."

Dr. Chu smiled. "You two really did your research."

"We wanted to be ready," Katy said.

"In case the cubs came to the nursery and they needed our help."

"Can I take their picture?" Micah asked the keeper.

"Only if you promise to send me a copy," Jennie said.

Micah pulled his camera from his pocket. "Deal."

"Look, Lulu is nursing the cubs," Javier said.

Dr. Chu wrote some notes in a chart. "Perfect. She's a good mama."

"Does this mean the cubs won't be going to the nursery? Because Lulu

doesn't need any help?" Katy asked her.

"That's right. They don't need to," the vet answered. "Thanks for being on standby."

Javier smiled. "That's our job at the nursery. To be prepared . . . and hope that we're not needed." He turned to Katy. "I'm sorry things didn't turn out the way you wanted."

"Actually, they did," she said. "I know what I said last week, but I changed my mind. The cubs belong with their mother."

"It would have been cool to feed a baby tiger," Micah said as they left the building. "But at least I got to take some pictures!"

CHAPTER 5

Picture Perfect

Sunday morning, Micah was eating cereal when his father handed him the phone. "Phone call for you. It's Katy."

Micah swallowed a mouthful of cereal. "Hello?"

"Have you seen it?" Katy squealed.

"What?"

"The zoo website. Go look at it, now!"

"Hold on." Micah put the phone

on speaker so his dad could hear. He raced out of the room and returned with the family laptop. He typed in the zoo's web address. A photo filled the screen. It was Lulu cuddling her cubs. "I took that picture! That's the one I sent to the keeper."

His father read the headline. "Zoo Welcomes Two Tiger Cubs." Then he pointed at the screen. "There's your name!"

"'Photo by Micah Draper,'" Micah read, grinning from ear to ear.

Katy's voice came over the speaker. "Congratulations!"

"Thanks!" Micah pushed aside his cereal bowl. "I can't wait to go back to the zoo. I wonder what our next assignment will be?"

THINK ABOUT IT

 Javier says that the nursery must always be well-stocked. What supplies would you order if you were setting up a zoo nursery?

 After talking to her mother, Katy is confused. She wants to take care of a baby tiger. But she wants Lulu to be healthy too. What would you want to happen?

Katy and Micah learned a lot about baby tigers. Research your favorite animal baby. How big is it? What does it eat? What else did you learn?

ABOUT THE AUTHOR

Brenda Scott Royce is the author of more than twenty books for adults and children. Animals are her favorite subject to write about. She has worked as a chimpanzee keeper at an animal sanctuary and traveled on wildlife expeditions to Africa and South America. In her free time, she helps injured birds as a volunteer with SoCal Parrot Rescue.

ABOUT THE ILLUSTRATOR

Joseph Wilkins is an illustrator living and working in the seaside town of Brighton, England. A graduate of Falmouth College of Arts in Cornwall, Joseph has spent the last fifteen years forging a successful freelance career. When not drawing, he can be found messing around with bicycles or on the beach with his family.

DOGGIE DAYCARE 🐶
IS OPEN FOR BUSINESS!

Join siblings Shawn and Kat Choi as they start their own pet-sitting service out of their San Francisco home. Every dog they meet has its own special personality, sending the kids on fun (and furry) adventures all over the city!

"Shawn and Kat are supported by a diverse cast in which readers of many colors can see themselves reflected. Problem-solvers and dog lovers alike will pounce on this series." —*Kirkus Reviews*

DOGGIE DAYCARE — Barking **Bella** — BY CAROL KIM — ILLUSTRATED BY COURTNEY GODBEY

DOGGIE DAYCARE 🐾 — Most Valuable **Puppy** — BY CAROL KIM — ILLUSTRATED BY FELIA HANAWATA

DOGGIE DAYCARE — Blue Ribbon **Pup** — BY CAROL KIM — ILLUSTRATED BY FELIA HANAWATA

DOGGIE DAYCARE — Library **Buddy** — BY CAROL KIM — ILLUSTRATED BY FELIA HANAWATA

DOGGIE DAYCARE — Muddy **Mutt** — BY CAROL KIM — ILLUSTRATED BY COURTNEY GODBEY

DOGGIE DAYCARE — Dog Sled **Star** — BY CAROL KIM — ILLUSTRATED BY FELIA HANAWATA

DOGGIE DAYCARE — Tank's Forever **Home** — BY CAROL KIM — ILLUSTRATED BY COURTNEY GODBEY

DOGGIE DAYCARE — One Trick **Puppy** — BY CAROL KIM — ILLUSTRATED BY COURTNEY GODBEY